PUBLISHED BY DS PRODUCTIONS

ISBN: 9798596754797

BULLETS FLY IN THE YELLOWSTONE MOUNTAINS

GENE TURNEY

DEDICATION

This novel, as are all my novels and everything I do, is dedicated to Cheryl, my children, grandchildren, nieces, nephews, cousin Pat, and other in-laws and outlaws and many friends encouragement. Without the faith and encouragement of so many, this book would not exist. With great appreciation, I acknowledge the people who have provided invaluable assistance to the development of this particular novel.

PREFACE

After the explorers discovered the Yellowstone Mountains, the reports of the grandeur and beauty served as a lure to attract those wanting to find a new life or to simply start their life in an exciting new territory. There were many obstacles to overcome, not the least being battles with a warlike culture, troubles from miscreants of all types and just life in general.

1.

Bill Taylor stopped at Fort Rice to resupply. He had been traveling for several weeks, and he wanted to be prepared to go into the mountain country, plus Grandy and Lou needed a rest. Grandy earned the name because as horses go, he turned out to be one Grand horse. Standing at fifteen hands, Bill kept Grandy's red coat shining. The mule had been named Lou since his earliest days. Bill bought Lou from a Kentucky farmer who decided to move into town. The fellow had tried to keep Lou, but the yard did not provide the mule with much room to roam. Bill learned of the possibility of buying Lou as he left town headed for the mountains.

Bill stood a little over six feet tall. His shoulders were broad and he had a slim waist. He appeared to be able to handle any physical situation that might arise. He left his home farm in Kentucky because he had gotten into some trouble due to his tendency to be quick to anger. He had a fight in town and he bested the man handily. It seems as though the man had decided Bill needed a good fight and goaded him into it. It just so happened that the man Bill had bested turned out to be the son of the local sheriff. The sheriff saw everything that happened and he arrested Bill for fighting while the other fellow walked away laughing. After they went inside the sheriff's office, Bill learned that he would not be arrested if he left town. That suited Bill because he wanted to get to Yellowstone.

Bill had been reading about the explorations in the Yellowstone area and he thought the territory would be the frontier that he needed. Bill liked the solitude and he thought maybe he could get his temper under control in the mountains.

Bill purchased buckskin shirts and pants. He bought plenty of wool socks and he also forced himself to buy two pairs of moccasins. Boots had been the order for Bill since he could walk. He would have to learn how to walk with the moccasins because when he put them on, he felt like he was walking in his bare feet. He reloaded his possible bag with plenty of things he would need such as needles and thread. He purchased several strands of beads of various colors so he would have something to trade.

After he had arrived at the fort, Bill became friends with a fellow traveler by the name of Henry Cockran. Henry had no desire to go to the mountains, he just wanted to get to Oregon which meant he would have to go through or around mountains.

Over supper one evening Henry asked Bill if he had noticed the activity at the fort.

"I have been to a bunch of these army forts, and I can tell you that something is about to happen. They have lined up wagons all over the place, and the troops are acting like they are getting ready to leave. I know about George Custer. I have read about him in the papers. Trouble seems to follow him around. He is here and he has been hustling around this fort like a banty rooster chasing a bunch of hens."

"I wonder if they are getting ready for an Indian war or something," Bill replied. "I wish they would quit that stuff and let this country settle down."

One of the army lieutenants happened to be walking near their camp and he heard the two men talking.

"Are you fellows looking for work? We are hiring scouts and guides for an expedition into Yellowstone. If you want to go, talk to Colonel Stanley. You will find him at the tent where the flag poles are located. We are leaving pretty soon, and we should be back by August or September. It should be some easy money. We are escorting railroad engineers and surveyors so they can find a way to lay track through here so the trains can run. Come on with us if you can."

The lieutenant walked on past the camp. Henry looked at Bill, "What do you think? We can make some money while we head out west of here. I think we should talk to them."

"You heard him say they are coming back here. I don't want to come back to this place. If I scouted for them, I would leave them at Yellowstone. If they are alright with that, I think I could stand some entertainment."

Both men appeared at Colonel Stanley's tent the next morning. After interviewing the two, the Colonel told them to go to the company bursar and give their information. They were being hired as civilians. They had told the Colonel they would scout, but when they reached Yellowstone, they would continue on their journeys. Colonel Stanley did not have any problem with their plans.

As they gave their information to the bursar so they could get paid, Henry heard Bill tell the clerk that he wanted his pay sent to a ranch in Texas.

"I heard you set your pay to go to a ranch in Texas. Who do you know in that place?" asked Henry.

"My brother Charlie Taylor has a place there. Our uncle runs the bank in a little town nearby. That is where I want my money to be sent. I may never pick it up, but at least it will be somewhere safe," laughed Bill.

"Well, I sent my money back home. My wife is taking care of our children and she is waiting for me to find a place in Oregon. I am anxious to get there and send for them. Maybe that train track will be in by that time and she can come on the train."

Bill and Henry were assigned to a group of scouts. They made number five and six of the group. They were told they would ride two miles apart and if any scout found things out of the ordinary like a large number of horses, or if they saw anything like Indians, they were to return to report their findings to the leader. The fellow in charge of their bunch of scouts went by the name of Lieutenant Brush. There were four other scouting units and they were made up mostly of Indians.

Bill had just celebrated his twenty-third birthday. He stood much taller and much more robust than the other scouts. They appeared as though they had missed many meals, but they were not bothered in the least about it. All of the scouts took around at the chow line. The food turned out to be tolerable, but Bill and Henry thought they could cook better than those in charge of feeding the soldiers.

Most of the scouts camped closely in their group, however, Henry had convinced Lieutenant Brush there would be an advantage to having scouts camp some distance away from the soldier encampment.

Brush approved the idea as long as Bill and Henry checked in with him in the mornings and evenings.

2.

Henry Cochran and Bill Taylor slopped through the country. They had been away from the fort for seventeen days, and it had rained for fourteen of those days. Three or four heavy rainfalls happened during those days, and very little progress had been recorded by the troops. There were over two hundred wagons on the expedition and nearly every one of them had been stuck axle-deep in the mud. Soldiers would unload the five thousand pound load, get the wagon out of the muddy hole, and then the wagon would be reloaded. The situation required a herculean effort just to get the wagons moving. Some of the wagons were made by the Charter Oak Wagon Company and those wagons could take a beating. Some of the other wagons, however, required constant maintenance and a crew of wagon mechanics stayed busy making repairs on those old wagons. The Charter Oak wagons carried vital materials such as food and clothing for the soldiers. The other wagons were loaded with forage for livestock and hardware for the bivouacs.

Bill and Henry scouted north of the wagon trail. Early one morning they found an advance party and the railroad engineers. They had become stranded after a hail storm blew through their area the night before. Bill and Henry had dealt with the heavy rain and were unaware of a hail storm. The soldiers, engineers, and the horses and mules were all a confused bunch. The wagons had been damaged so severely they could not move forward. Horses and mules had suffered the onslaught of hard hailstones the size of a man's fist. Several of the horses had been knocked unconscious by the hail.

Soldiers and engineers were sheltered under their wagons, but some of the soldiers were battered by hail. One man had several large knots on his head from his dashing out in the storm to retrieve a frightened horse.

Bill took the report of the storm damage and the location of the railroad engineers back to the camp where he gave the information to Brush. He had to wait for a detail to be put together so he could lead them to the site of the damage. A crew of wagon mechanics loaded a wagon with spare parts. Several medics loaded an ambulance with a stock of supplies including rations for the men. A vet rode alongside Bill. He asked enough questions to learn the condition of the horses and mules.

A day passed while preparations were made and the group left the main camp early the next morning in a deluge of rain. When they arrived at the location where the hail storm blew through, soldiers set about to start making things right.

Bill and Henry continued to scout the area two miles north and west of the wagon trail. They found it difficult to report back to Brush every evening and finally received permission to report only if they found something out of the ordinary.

The rain stopped and several days passed with the temperatures starting to soar. By late summer, the expedition had reached the mouth of Sunday Creek, a tributary to the Yellowstone.

"We are getting close to where I feel like dropping off this scouting stuff. Those mountains are calling my name," Bill told Henry.

"I am not ready yet. Brush told me that we were to scout west of here ahead of Custer's bunch, and you know that means we will see trouble," Henry replied.

The two scouts topped a knoll to see a band of Sioux warriors traveling across the trail Bill and Henry intended to travel. One of the warriors spotted the two men who thought they had found a hiding spot at the edge of the forest.

A shot rang out from one of the Indians. The bullet thudded into the tree trunk about thirty feet in front of Henry. Another shot followed the first one.

"That did not sound like an old flintlock," Henry exclaimed. "I think that was one of those Winchester repeaters. I believe the ball has opened."

Following orders previously given them, the two scouts retreated from their position without firing. Soldiers started showing up and they learned that Custer's column had heard the two shots that were fired at the scouts.

A skirmish line quickly formed by Custer's troops and a volley of fire distracted the pursuing Indians. While the current attack paused briefly, soldiers were able to scatter and establish a perimeter.

"You wanted a party, so here it is," shouted Bill. He leveled his Sharps rifle and fired into the attacking warriors. The troops had scattered to points where it took every eighth man to hold the horses when the soldiers dismounted. A separate company of mounted soldiers retreated further into the forest.

After a three-hour-long back and forth between the soldiers and the Indian warriors, the mounted troops broke out from their wooded positions and flanked the Indians. The Indians realized retreat was the only option. The Sioux forces fled upriver with Custer's men in pursuit. The pursuit lasted about four miles before the troops returned to camp without the opportunity to engage the Indians.

3.

Frank Taylor liked the bank to open before nine in the morning. Since he had become president of the bank, he took it upon himself to make sure the bank opened early, and he could be found unlocking the doors early every morning.

Little Billy stopped by the post office to gather the morning mail and he carried the mail across the street to the bank in a saddlebag. He plopped the saddlebag on Frank's desk and went about his duties as vice president of the bank. It took Little Billy and two others to make up the staff of the little bank. The bank was little only in its size. Since Frank had retired from his big bank in New York, the financial situation had stabilized and the bank grew in money wealth, and property.

"Little Billy, I think you probably know where your father in law lives, don't you?" Frank asked.

"Guess I do. We were there for dinner last night,"

"There is a letter here from the United States Military that needs to be taken out to Charlie. I will watch things here while you run the letter out."

"Sure thing, I will get right on it. What is the letter about anyway?" asked Billy.

"I do not know. It is in a sealed official-looking envelope and it is kind of fat and heavy, so there is something in there."

Billy walked to his house at the edge of Live Oak Springs, saddled his horse, and rode out to the Taylor ranch in a short time.

Charlie Taylor sat in a rocking chair on the front porch of his ranch house. His wife Lizzie sat nearby. She worked on some needlework while Charlie enjoyed his morning coffee.

"Lizzie, look who is here. Billy, get down off that horse and come have some coffee with us," said Charlie.

"I sure would like to do that Mr. Taylor, but I am supposed to deliver this mail to you and get back to the bank." Billy handed the letter to Charlie as he reached over the porch railing.

"Stay there just a bit, I may have to respond to this, Billy. It would be really handy if you could take the response back to town for me." Charlie used his pocket knife to open the top of the envelope. He looked inside and then looked up at Billy. "Yes sir, you better get down from there. I will have something for you to take back to town."

Lizzie looked on with interest, "what is it, Charlie? I hope it is something good."

Charlie dumped the contents of the envelope onto a table next to his chair. Cash fell to the table along with an official-looking letter.

"Lizzie, this letter says that my brother Bill has been scouting for the military, and this cash is his pay. He has instructed them to send the money to me so I can put it in the bank for him. Goodness, there must be close to three hundred dollars here. I have not heard from Bill since I left Kentucky years ago. We have written to each other a little, but I had no idea that he would scout for the army. He always wanted to go to the mountains as ole John did. Billy, I will get this fixed up so you can take it to the bank and open an account for Bill Taylor."

Charlie went inside the ranch house to the office where he conducted all the ranch business. He found a deposit book and filled out a slip for the money. He included a note to his uncle Frank to open a bank account for Bill Taylor. He walked back out to the porch and handed Little Billy an envelope with the money and the note.

Frank expressed surprise at the note from Charlie. He had lost track of his nephew Bill. Frank had advanced his career in New York and took no time off to keep in touch with his family. His brother and sister-in-law were killed and he had made arrangements with his sister to take care of the boys. He provided financial support to make sure their upbringing happened comfortably. He reflected on what little he knew of Bill Taylor and hoped him well as he set up a bank account for his nephew. Frank thought he would one day see Bill when he comes to collect his money.

4.

"I guess the banquet is over," Bill loaded his sharps rifle. "I think ole Custer needs to take his troops out for some shooting practice. I do not think they can claim they hit a single Indian in three hours of trying.'

"Well, I sure did not hit anybody with all that lead I threw over there either," replied Henry. "I am thinking about going over there and digging it out of those trees. We can heat it and make some more cartridges. There may be enough over there to last us through the fall."

Lieutenant Brush walked down the scrimmage line talking with the soldiers in the trench. He stopped when he reached Bill Taylor and Henry Cochran.

"My scouts are supposed to hunt and find. I did not hear the word shoot in there anywhere. Why are my two best scouts hiding behind these trees? Boys, we need you out there looking for the dangers ahead. We heard the shots you fellows drew and thought somebody shot at buffalo. You are two lucky fellows to get out of that scrap without being shot," Brush had his chest puffed out and both hands on his belt. He had not been a part of the skirmish.

"I guess you could say the same for those fellows that ran at us. I do not think scaring them with lead does a bit of good. They finally figured there were more of us than there were of them and they scadoodled. Nary a one ran off with any of our lead and we had all afternoon to give them some," replied Henry.

Bill Taylor and Henry Cochran made a name for themselves as scouts. They managed to find signs that other scouts had missed or thought little of. One, in particular, kept Custer's forces from being trapped in an ambush. The troops had been lured to a skirmish that developed on each of the banks of the Yellowstone River. A small contingent of Sioux began the skirmish by shooting across the river. While soldiers dismounted and began to return fire, Taylor and Cochran alerted officers about a large group collecting behind a ridge. It became obvious the warriors intended to trap the soldiers.

Colonel Stanley moved artillery into the area and disbursed the Indians on the ridge. The distance from one bank of the Yellowstone to the other meant there were no casualties. The Indian bow and arrow fell way short, and the soldiers had difficulty finding someone to get into their sights on their rifles.

A few days later, scouts Taylor and Cochran gave warning of a large contingent of Indians in the path of Colonel Stanley's expedition. Once again, Custer volunteered to move his cavalry forward. A squabble began with Custer's troops and over a thousand warriors. Colonel Stanley arrived to provide reinforcements. The sharp skirmish lasted for several days and the Indians finally left the territory to the surveyors.

"I tell you what, Taylor. I am getting worn out with these battles that we seem to find ourselves in. I am ready to call this little trip done and head back to the fort," Henry leaned back on his saddle which he had put on the ground when they stopped for camp. Campfires showed up all over the countryside as the sun began to set. Both scouts were weary of the saddle and the battle.

Lieutenant Brush came to their camp and asked them if they were ready to get back to Fort Rice.

"The engineers have finished their work. We are at the mouth of the Little Big Horn. Some of our stores will be headed down the river and we will travel light, so our journey to the fort should come in short order. We will need you two scouts to continue your work, but it is doubtful you will encounter any more troubles because we are taking a more southern route which will move us away from Indian Territory."

Henry let out a little yell of relief. "I am sure glad to hear that news. I am ready to find my blankets and have a good sleep. I would guess our worries are just a little less."

"I think I may decide to go on into the mountains from here," Bill looked to the northwest mountain range.

"You will probably run into a lot of trouble going that direction," Brush replied. "We know Sitting Bull is up there. He is mad at us because he thinks we chased off all of the buffalo they were hunting," Brush laughed, "We probably did chase them off after we got enough for us to eat. I do not think the buffalo will stay gone very long. It was just another reason to be mad at us."

Bill studied Brush's thoughts about traveling northwest.

"You are probably right there are a lot of Sioux up in there, but I will be traveling by myself without a bunch to make a lot of noise. I think I can manage to get through just fine. These wagons and troops are loud when they get underway.

We could scout four miles away and still hear all the banging of the wagons and every once in a while we could hear men talking. We could not make out what was said, but we could hear them. I do not think you people realize how much racket you make."

"Well, you are probably right that one man could make it through where a bunch of us would start some sort of shooting match with them. We plan to rest up here for a couple of days before we start back. Taylor, let me know when you head out for the hills so I can put a scratch by your name. You will not be called a deserter because you are a civilian worker, and I know you had talked your plan over with the Colonel before we left Fort Rice."

"That is right I did talk with him and he said he would be fine with me leaving out when I got ready. I want my pay sent where I had told that fellow back at the fort," said Bill.

"Some money has already been sent," said the Lieutenant as he narrowed his eyes to try to read in his little ledger book that he kept in his pocket. "I will make sure the rest gets sent when we get back. I may not be able to visit with you again before we leave, but I want to tell you, two fellows, you are some of the best scouts we have had. We found out a couple of those Indian scouts we had were not working in our best interest and nearly got one of our columns wiped out. You two men did yourself proud and on behalf of the Colonel, the United States thanks you."

5.

Before daylight the next morning, Bill Taylor had saddled Grandy and packs were tied on Lou. "I think I need to come up with a better name for you old mule. Lou does not fit. I can't figure where that fellow came up with the name, and you do not answer to it anyway. I am gonna think about that while we are on the trail to the mountains."

Bill mounted his horse. Campfire smoke stayed low to the ground and there was little wind to move it around. The smell of burning pine wood was strong in the air. Grandy waded through the smoke to the tent where Lieutenant Brush had a pot of coffee boiling. Brush put a small stick of wood on the fire and sparks flew up in the air.

Bill stopped Grandy short of coming close to the fire. He touched his hand to his hat, and he saw Brush acknowledge with a touch to his hat.

Grandy turned and Bill Taylor left the military camp headed for the mountains of Yellowstone.

After crossing the river, a meadow stretched out for about a mile. Not wanting to be in open territory, Bill wanted to get into the forest as soon as possible. He spotted a stand of pine trees nearby that would lead around to the dense forest. As Grandy picked a way through the deadfall, Lou kept tugging on the lead rope that had been tied to the back of the saddle. During a stop, Bill untied the lead rope, knowing the mule would follow Grandy through the woods.

As they reached the more dense wooded forest, Bill could hardly hear Grandy's hoof muffled on the pine bed on the ground. Lou seemed to be able to find just the right spot to step that would snap a small piece of wood. The trees seemed to act like a deadening force against the sound. After several hours of riding in the dense forest, Bill stopped for a cold lunch. He could not tell the location of the sun because the rays did not reach the forest floor, but his stomach told him that noon approached. Even though the late summer months had brought searing temperatures, the forest temperature stayed on the cool side.

While the horse and mule rested nearby, Bill sat on the ground and leaned his back against a giant tree. He watched the squirrels scamper from one tree to the next. Birds were everywhere in the forest. He spotted a marten running across the ground. He went up a tree trunk and got on the backside of the tree out of Bill's sight. While traveling through the forest, Bill sought the solitude the trees provided. At his first camp, he realized the forest contained a tremendous amount of life if one would just stop and watch.

Bill saddled Grandy and loaded his packs on Lou to continue his journey to the mountains. Again, he let the horse pick a trail through the dense forest and Lou followed along.

After several hours of slow walking in the woods, Bill saw a large park that started at the edge of the forest. It stretched along the edge for about a mile and the forest picked up again about a mile across the park. The sun had begun to lean down toward the horizon, but there would be enough time to see if he could hunt up a deer.

Bill made camp a hundred yards back from the park. He liked the cover of the forest. After hobbling Grandy and Lou, he took his Sharps rifle and walked along the edge of the forest to see if he could spot deer grazing in the park. He had become accustomed to wearing the moccasins and he thought he could be stealthy enough to surprise a deer. He stepped carefully to avoid any little sticks or branches that would signal the excellent hearing the deer possessed.

Bill heard a snap, and then a noise like someone made a grunt. His eyes had become accustomed to the darkness of the forest, so he looked around for the source of the noise. He spotted three Indians who were hunting. They had spotted a herd of deer and they were focused on closing the distance so they could get a shot.

Bill watched from a safe distance as the three Indians dropped to the ground and quietly crawled to within a hundred feet of two bucks and four doe. The wind blew their scent into the forest, and the deer heard no disturbance in their surroundings. The three hunters have spread twenty yards apart, and they worked in concert as they loaded their bows and all three let the arrows fly at the same time. Bill could hear the noise the arrows made as they sailed through the air toward their targets. Each arrow struck home and the three deer fell to the ground. The hunters jumped up in celebration and ran to their prey. They made quick work of getting the deer ready to carry back to their village.

Bill rested behind the tree that he thought hid him from the view of the hunters when he heard a thunk and he felt the tree shake. That sound came from an arrow striking the tree. Bill had been spotted by the hunting party.

He looked to his left to see one of the Indians trying to sneak back into the forest to get behind him. He looked out and did not see any movement in the park and that meant the other two hunters were somewhere to his right. Bill dropped to the ground and crawled past several trees to a short stand of juniper. The little bush had no chance of survival in the forest, but it was trying it's best to grow. Bill looked through the little branches to see the hunter that was sneaking to his left still looking in the general direction of the tree he had just left. The hunter stood, loaded an arrow, and fired at the tree again. After the arrow missed the tree, the hunter started directing the other two in the direction where Bill had last been seen.

The hunter caught a glimpse of the barrel of the Sharps rifle as Bill started to get into position to fire a shot. The hunter yelled and started on a run to where Bill had hidden. The shot from the rifle hit home and dropped the hunter. The report of the rifle shot seemed to be very loud in the forest. Bill stood and looked for the other two hunters. They had fled at the hearing of the shot. They ran back to the park and grabbed two deer carcasses and ran south away from Bill along the edge of the woods. Eventually, they ducked into the woods and Bill lost sight of them.

Since a deer had been left behind by the hunters, Bill thought he might as well take advantage. He picked the deer up and straddled it over his shoulders. He decided he needed to find a better location for his camp to get well away from the park and the area where he had shot the hunter. He made quick work of saddling Grandy, repacking Lou, and starting for a new campsite.

6.

After working his way to the northwest of the park, Bill found a large lake. While he did not have any maps of Yellowstone, he felt the last mountain he had topped put him in the caldera. The lake stretched as far as he could see and it lay several miles wide.

Bill followed a deer trail that led to the edge of the lake. He stopped before leaving the protection of the woods so that he could view the surroundings. The sight was breathtaking. The heat of the summer had not burned the grass to blonde, it remained a beautiful bright green. Flowers spread over the areas between the water and the woods. This looked like the ideal place to put up a long term camp.

Bill stretched the tarp between two trees for shelter. Pine boughs made a good soft spot for his blankets. He started a fire to cook the venison and he walked to the lake to get water to boil for coffee.

As he stepped out of the edge of the woods, Bill noticed the body of an Indian. The man had lain on his left side, and when Bill approached, a swarm of flies took off from the man's right thigh.

Thinking the Indian had died, Bill walked around to see the front of the man. The Indian's eyes were open.

"You scared the flies away. I think they were having a meal on my leg," the Indian spoke very good English. "I guess you are here to finish with me. Why aren't you wearing the blue coat like the one that shot me?"

"I am not with them. How bad off are you?" asked Bill.

"I did not think I had been hurt bad. I got here to get a fish and my horse decided to go home. I have not been able to get fish. I am hungry and I need to look after where that bullet hit my leg," said the Indian.

Bill helped the man to a sitting position. He went to the lake and got water so the wound could be cleaned. Bill had no way to get the bullet out of the man's leg, and he was certain infection or gangrene would set in if that bullet did not come out.

The Indian cleaned the wound and wrapped Bill's bandanna around the leg to stop the bleeding.

"That bullet needs to come out of there. I do not have anything that would get it out, though."

The Indian held up a rifle slug, "I have taken it out. I thought maybe those flies might be after it."

The Indian held up a big knife with a blood-covered blade.

Bill knew he looked at a tough warrior. He hoped that if he ever had a bullet wound that he could get help to pull out the bullet, but here sat a man that took it out himself.

"I came here to put my leg in the mud. I think the bone is broken and I need the mud to heal my leg. I will dig a hole next to the water if you can help me over there."

"What is your name?"

The Indian pointed to his white hair, "My name is Hotah. I am chief of the people you call the Cow Creek Sioux. My name means white. I have had white hair since baby."

"My name is Bill," he replied as he lifted Hotah by picking him up under both arms.

"Bill, this will not work. I cannot stand and I cannot walk. Just drag Hotah over to the mud."

Bill struggled to pull the man through the grass and weeds to the edge of the water where the mud became soft.

"This is fine. Leave me here. I will let the mud heal my leg. I will catch fish and make a fire," Hotah looked up at Bill.

Bill knew the Sioux tribe had attacked Custer's soldiers and lead passed back and forth between the two sides. However, Bill could not just walk away from an injured man who needed help. Hotah must have been one of the warriors that attacked the troops. Yes, he knew a soldier would have put the Indian out of his misery, but the Indians had not done anything to Bill. And, he planned to live in the mountains. He would stay as far away from them as possible and he would regard them as a danger to his survival, but the man before him did not meet those criteria.

Bill nodded at Hotah, he walked to the lake, filled his bucket with fresh water, and headed back to his camp. He intended to leave the Indian be and go on about his business.

Bill's campfire had burned down to red coals. He put the water on to boil for coffee and he sharpened several green branches to hold strips of venison over the fire. While he cooked his evening meal, he could hear the Indian chanting. Bill knew the Indian had nothing with which to catch fish, and he wondered how he could build a fire at the edge of the lake when the needed wood was out of his reach.

7.

After enjoying a cup of coffee, Bill picked up several of the sticks of venison. On his walk to the lake, he gathered small wood to set next to Hotah so he could build a fire. When he reached where the Indian had buried himself up to his waist in the mud, Bill handed Hotah one of the sticks with venison dangling on the end. Hotah nodded a thank you and started eating.

Bill dropped the wood in a stack next to the Indian.

"Why do you do this? I am on the other side. I do not believe I would do this for you. Your hair would be mine if I found you this way."

"Maybe that is why I am doing this. You think you can do all this yourself. I think I can help you. I don't want your white hair, and after the moon leaves, you will not want my hair either." Bill pointed to his shock of black hair.

"We will see when the sun rises," replied Hotah.

Bill cut a few long branches so Hotah would have something he could use for fishing. He left them with the Indian and went back to his camp. Grandy and Lou had been hobbled to keep them close. They were grazing peacefully in a small meadow nearby.

Bill had every intention of making his bed and getting to sleep. A long day had come to an end. Sounds of chanting continued into the night as Bill dozed off.

The sun edged near the horizon as Bill rekindled the small campfire. He had water left in the pot, so he decided on a quick cup of coffee. He could hear Hotah continuing with his chanting near the water of the lake. Occasionally, Hotah would let out a yell, and after a few moments, the yelling took on a serious nature.

Bill grabbed his rifle and walked to the edge of the forest. He saw Hotah waving his arms and shouting at something to the left of where the Indian had buried himself in the mud. In his left hand, Hotah had one of the branches Bill had left for him to use for fishing. He used the branch to fend off an animal that Bill could not see. When he stepped around the tree and into the open, Bill saw a black bear crouched beyond the reach of the branch. Hotah yelled at the bear, but the yelling did not scare the small bear away.

While a black bear can become large, the one threatening Hotah looked to be a young bear and on the small side. The bear looked at Hotah with curiosity and watched him swing the branch to try to keep the bear at a safe distance.

Hotah had been swinging that heavy branch for quite some time and Bill could see the strength leaving his arms. The bear must have noticed it also, and simply waited until a safe attack could be launched.

Hotah put the branch on the ground and the bear stood up tall. The end seemed to be near for Hotah.

The shot from Bill's rifle rang loud in the forest. Birds flew up from the trees. Leaves fell from the tree near where Bill stood. The bullet followed the true course and smacked into the head of the attacking bear. Hotah watched the bear rock forward and backward before falling on its back. Hotah turned toward the water and calmly started chanting again. Bill had no idea the meaning of the chanting, but he hoped Hotah chanted a thank you to the heavens because his life had just been saved.

As Bill walked to the water's edge, Hotah turned and smiled at Bill.

"You talk truth. The sun has risen. I do not want your hair," Hotah gestured toward the bear. "I will take care of that bear for my friend. Put him here and let me work."

Again, Bill had a struggle trying to drag the three hundred pound bear to the spot Hotah had indicated. When the bear had been deposited to Hotah's satisfaction, he drew out his knife and started the skinning process. Bill started toward his camp.

"Before you go, look at the tree yonder," Hotah pointed to the tree near where Bill had found him. A Winchester rifle leaned against the trunk of the tree. Bill remembered picking the rifle up when he walked around in front of Hotah to determine if he had died. "You would be a friend again," Hotah fell silent.

On his way back to his camp, Bill could hear the chanting. He thought maybe he should move into the forest a little further. That chanting had kept him from having a good sleep. After a breakfast of venison and hardtack left from his days with the military, the rain started.

At first, the clouds let a drizzle fall, but that became an indicator of what was to come. A hard rain fell for a few minutes, and then the drizzle started again. Bill could see the dense fog over the huge lake of water. He saw Hotah still working on the bear. He had removed enough hide to try to make a shelter from the rain, but it did not prove effective.

Bill cut four sturdy branches that were about four feet long. He took them to where Hotah healed his leg in the mud. The soft ground gave easily as Bill pushed the four branches down into the mud. Bill started collecting other branches and pine boughs from the forest. When he returned, he made a shelter over Hotah so he would not get drenched in the rain. Hotah helped by arranging the branches and boughs that formed the covering. Bill pushed more branches into the ground and three sides were closed in.

Bill looked inside the shelter to see Hotah trying to make things comfortable. He had buried himself almost to his waist in the mud. Hotah had some upper body movement, but the mud would continue to dry and form a cast around the broken leg. Enough room had been left in the front of the shelter so Hotah could continue working on the freshly killed bear.

"You must shout when you come," Hotah patted the rifle that lay by his side.

Back at his camp, Bill began to wonder why he had decided to stop his venture to help this Indian. Not too long ago, the men were shoulder to shoulder and were being attacked by Indian warriors. He wanted to come to the mountains for solitude.

Bill's young mind had convinced him that he would leave all of the ruckus behind and that he would find peace in the mountains. Maybe if he continued on his journey and sought the silence of the forest and the beauty the mountains held he could rid himself of the images of battle. Bill cleaned his pistol and his rifle. He learned early on to keep his weapons clean and in good condition.

The supply of venison began to run low since Bill shared his food with Hotah. The Indian had given him some bear meat, but the taste did not fit his pallet. The meat would serve as a meal in desperate times, but Bill preferred venison, elk, grouse, turkey, or anything that would be considered ordinary fare. Bear meat did not fit in that menu. The heavy bearskin would certainly come in handy during the winter months, however.

Before sleep overcame him, Bill had decided he needed to move on. While no clock ticked the minutes and hours away, Bill felt he had fallen behind in his plans to make his home in the Yellowstone Mountains. The location where he camped would be a good place to call home, but it appeared to him that other humans thought the same thing. There were too many Indians around.

The morning chores this day included breaking camp. Bill filled packs and covered the area where he camped with pine leaves. He had Grandy saddled, and the packs were loaded on Lou.

"I have not come up with a good name for you yet, Lou, but, I will continue to think on it, and I will find a name that fits."

Hotah had started chanting again well before sunrise. The chanting must have had something to do with calling in the medicine spirits to help with the healing of the broken bone in his leg. If that were indeed the case, Bill thought Hotah should be up and walking in a day or two.

"I am coming in from behind, so hold your fire," Bill shouted at Hotah. The shelter that had been built around him did provide relief from the weather, but Hotah could not see an approaching enemy.

"I heard you before you put out your campfire. Your horses make much noise. You have two, and why do you call one by the name of Lou? I would never call my horse Lou. Have you seen my horse? He is brown with white on him. A good horse for someone with the name of Hotah. He left me when I fell under the big tree. I will need my horse when I leave this place and go to my home."

"Where is your home, Hotah?" asked Bill.

"It is two moons from here," Hotah pointed east. Bill felt relief because he intended to head in the opposite direction.

"Where is your village?" Hotah asked.

"I have not found it yet. I am looking for the place so I can find peace," replied Bill.

"You will find that to be a long journey, my friend. In my village, there is no peace. We have battles to plan. Other people want our place. We will not give up," said Hotah.

"I do not want your place. I want a place where there are no other people. I will find that place and it will be my home," Bill stood in front of Hotah's shelter. "It is time for me to go on my journey. I hope you get well soon."

"I have made you my friend because you put me here and built my house for me. I have made you my friend because you stopped the bear from having me for food. I wish you well on your journey and I hope you find your peace and take care of that horse you call Lou."

Bill mounted his saddle and turned to head west and into the forest. He had not traveled far before he discovered Hotah's horse grazing along the edge of the forest where the green grass continued to grow. Bill put a lead rope on the mustang and took the horse to where Hotah continued to chant. When the horse heard Hotah's voice, his ears pricked forward and he stepped up his pace in the direction of the shelter.

As he approached the shelter, Bill heard the ratcheting of a bullet in preparation for firing.

"I have found your horse," Bill shouted.

"I can tell because you make noise. It is not the same noise you made when you came," shouted Hotah.

Bill dismounted and led the horse to the shelter and handed Hotah the lead rope.

"I cannot use this," Hotah said while holding the rope out to Bill. "Take it from the horse. He will stay close and he will come when I call him."

Bill followed Hotah's instructions and the little mustang ambled to a patch of green grass.

The heat and the mosquitoes continued to intensify. Bill saw little spots of blood on Grandy's shoulder where a swarm of mosquitoes bit into the horse before he could swipe them away. Lou had been stomping on the ground with all four, he shook his head, and his tail had been busy swishing back and forth. The time had come for Bill to lay out a plan to get to a place where he could call it home.

8.

Several days of riding past and Bill found himself deep in the forest, and he was not sure of his location. He searched for a park or a meadow so that he could get a read on the sun and find his directions. He felt like he had been in the forest darkness for a long time, and his mind had started heading in dark directions as well. A small park finally showed itself. The grass grew green because there had been a weather event that caused a heavy downfall of trees. Grandy stepped over spruce and pine. Most of the logs sounded hollow, and some had deteriorated long ago. In the middle of the park, Bill found a spot where a spring-fed a stream that ran westward down to a bluff.

He set his packs in the cleared area and hobbled Grandy and Lou so they could enjoy the green grass. It would be a treat for them, and water trickled close by. Bill put together a small campfire for making coffee. The venison had played out long ago, and the hunting in the forest had not proven to be fruitful. Several animal trails led to the stream and he thought there might be some luck later in the day. Bill got a good read on the sun. He noticed the sun headed down and that meant late afternoon. He had been riding due west according to the sun position. A small compass had been accurate to keep Bill on a path that would eventually take him to the foothills of the mountains.

Bill had become accustomed to the silence in the forest. He picked up noises of the birds and squirrels and he had tried to learn from the songbirds. Bill decided to abandon that idea, all he could do was scare off a covey when he started whistling his version of the song. He recalled an entire flock of grackles taking flight when he tried the song of a mockingbird.

The sunshine felt good on Bill's face. He smiled as he closed his eyes and faced the sun to let the warm rays wash over him. It seemed like it had been a long time since he had enjoyed the sun. The season had begun to turn early fall. It would be a few weeks yet before leaves started turning, but Bill could feel a change in the weather.

Bill heard a loud ruckus in the woods and a big bull elk stomped out of the forest. He slung his head up and down and side to side to try to throw off a limb that had wedged in his horns. While the big bull would be better than what he had now, Bill reached for his rifle thinking that meat would not be very good.

He looked at a bull elk that had made it up in years. As he pulled his gun near, he saw a much smaller elk step out behind the old bull. Bill had the young elk in his sights and fired a shot that brought the elk down. He focused on the young elk so intently, he did not see the old bull elk head back into the woods for cover. Bill pulled the lever down on the Sharp's rifle to chamber another round. He discovered he had fired his last bullet. A search through all of the packs turned up three cartridges for the rifle. Taylor still had a six-shooter, and he had packed away plenty of ammunition for that gun, but he shorted himself on bullets for the long gun. While the six-shooter would certainly provide protection, Bill favored the Sharp's rifle because of its range. It would keep danger much further away than the little six-shooter. He realized he needed to find a place where he could get more supplies.

The meadow provided a convenient rest stop. Grandy began to put some weight on and Lou would look at Bill Taylor to let him know he planned to stay right where he was. Lou stood a little taller than Grandy and had larger muscles. Grandy had been built for speed, while Lou had been built for power. Lou knew all of that and used the strength to his advantage. He seemed to enjoy giving Taylor difficulty at times. When the packs were being cinched, Lou would suck in a lot of air. After the work with cinches ended, Lou would let out air and the cinches would be loose and hanging beneath the mule. Lou would turn in a direction to keep Taylor from noticing the cinch did not get tight. A long way down the trail, Bill would look back to make sure

Lou stayed close and he would see the packs leaning to one side or the other. Lou would raise his head and look at Bill as to say, "What? I don't think you did a good job with these packs."

Bill delighted in these imaginary conversations he would have with Grandy and Lou. He decided he better watch himself because if he carried on like that with folks around he could be put away.

While the camp in the meadow provided a nice respite, Bill decided he would leave the next day to try to find civilization. He had cleaned all of his eating tools and he carried a pot of water back to camp so he could make coffee. A shot rang out in the dusk. Bill felt the bullet hit the pot he held in his hand and when he held it up to see, water poured out of two holes in the pot. A second shot convinced Bill to hit the ground and see if he could make his way back to where his rifle lay.

"Ray, I think I got him. I do not see him anymore," the yell came from behind Bill.

"Keep your eye out. I do not see him either, but that does not mean he is dead. He could be just lying in the grass. Stay where you are and I will come around to you," came the reply. The man speaking seemed to be located to Bill's right shoulder. He crawled on his stomach and reached the camp. While he grabbed the Sharps rifle, he wondered how he could find the two men without poking his head up above the grass. Bill heard horses galloping to the right. He knew where a trail led around the park close to the edge of the woods, but that trail had a lot of deadfalls and a horse on a gallop would have trouble navigating.

The horse seemed to stop. Bill thought the two men had met up and he waited to see if they would move to the area where he fell. He had left the pot on the ground. It would be of no use with two holes blasted in the thing. The bullet went in one side and out the other.

The two men did not care how much noise they made as they walked toward Bill's campsite.

"I hope we find something to eat at that camp. We have not had anything to eat in three days. If you had not scared off those deer, we would be fat and sassy right now. My belly is gnawing on my backbone."

"Sam, you scared those deer your own self. It might have been that holler you let out when you saw them," answered Ray. "Where did that fellow fall?" Ray kicked the pot containing the two holes. "I see you did a mighty fine job of placing a couple of vents in this pot, but I don't see no meal ticket as you claimed him to be."

Both men were looking at the ground when the report of the Sharps rang out in the meadow. Bill used one of the three cartridges to shoot at the ground close to the pot. Sam and Ray were startled and they froze in their steps. Finally, Ray came to his senses.

"We are caught out here with no cover, Sam." Ray grabbed Sam by the arm and pulled him to the ground. "I am thinking you probably missed the man. I hope you have a plan because I sure don't."

Bill had enough killing lately. He sure did not want to die in the Yellowstone when he had not had the chance to get further along in his plan to make the mountains home. But, the two fellows seem to be intent on making sure he would not be able to breathe another day.

"Where is your elephant?" Bill yelled.

"What is he talking about, Ray? There are not any elephants in this country that I know of. Do you think there might be some out there somewhere?" ask Sam.

Ray yelled back, "What are you talking about. We do not have an elephant."

"Sorry boys, I thought you might be with the carnival. You make enough noise, and you need some practice in the shooting gallery. It is my mistake. I can put you both down, but I do not want to do that. What do you want?" yelled Bill.

"We need something to eat," yelled Sam.

"If you will put your guns away, I will let you into my camp. I have some good elk," Bill replied.

After Sam and Ray talked matters over in hushed talk, Ray asked if he could stand up. Bill agreed, but he told him that if he stood up with a gun, he would be dropping down with lead in him. Ray stood and held both arms out shoulder high to show he did not have a gun in his hand. He carried a six-shooter in a holster worn low on his hip.

Ray saw Bill sitting with the Sharps resting on one of his knees. He knew the man had a bead drawn on his chest.

"All right, we will be nice and friendly if you would let us in to take part in that banquet you have," said Ray.

Bill let them come to within about fifty feet of his camp when he made them stop and sit on the ground. He took some cooked elk meat and some cornbread to the two men.

"I would offer some coffee, but somebody put a couple of holes in my coffee pot," said Bill.

As he handed the food over, he told them to eat and then go back to where they came from.

"We cannot do that," said Sam. "Ray here is wanted by the law, and I have no business with them either."

"You have no business here with me, and I suggest you find your horses and head east. You will find plenty of game there and plenty of grass and water for your horses."

"That is fine with us, but where are you headed?" Ray asked.

Bill looked at his compass and then looked out toward the closest mountain.

"I am heading out of here and going northwest. I plan to travel to that mountain over there," Bill pointed to a mountain. The tree line stopped a good distance up the side of the mountain, and cold bare ground stretched from the tree line to the peak of the mountain.

"Since you gave us some food, I will give you some advice," Sam piped up. "You will run across a couple of rivers and you will hit some ground where there is an outfitter place. There are trappers all over that country over there, and those are people you do not want to mess with. We tried that beaver trapping, and that is not for us. That is where Ray got into some trouble.

One of those trappers decided to try to steal Ray's money. Ray did not have to kill the man, but he did it anyway."

"Now wait up here," Ray decided he needed to defend himself. "That trapper tried to hit me with a bunch of those beaver traps. He reared back and swung those things at my head. It was kill or be killed, and I still have my money."

"I am not interested in your history, but you say there is a supply store over there somewhere?" asked Bill.

"Yeah, you cannot miss it. There are trails all over the place that lead to it. It is run by an old cuss by the name of Trapper Kelly. You need to stay clear of him, too. He knows everything going on in the mountains, and he knew about Ray's hard times up there. I would just as soon you keep that you saw me and Ray in your pocket."

The two men found their horses where they had been tied before shots were taken at Bill. They headed east, following Bill's instructions.

Disappointed he had no pot to make coffee, Bill packed everything, saddled Grandy, and loaded Lou.

For some reason, Lou did not take to having the packs loaded. He tried several times to take a bite out of Bill.

"I know this has been a good place for you and Grandy to be lazy, but we have work to do and you better quit trying to bite," Bill pushed the mule's head around straight while he finished tying the packs.

Having only two bullets left for the rifle left Bill in bad enough shape, but to not have a pot to boil water turned out to be a downright terrible affair.

9.

Bill traveled for several days and missed his coffee every single morning. He began to think it would have been a better deal to plant the man that shot up his water pot.

Grandy and Lou made it easily across the two rivers and Bill found a spot where several trails joined into one. He knew he would be on the right track for finding the lodge. The horse and mule were both showing signs of tiring, so Bill made a camp in an area where there looked to have been plenty of activity. The ground showed signs of wagon tracks, and he found evidence the wagons had been circled. Tracks led west and Bill thought they were headed to the supply lodge. A small hill lay west of the campsite.

During the night, two scouts woke Bill. He had been drifting in and out of sleep, and he heard their approach several hundred yards away. They were on foot and did not present a danger to Bill, but he moved out of his blankets and away from his camp.

"Looks like somebody has set up camp here. We need to find him and let him know the wagons will be in here early in the morning. It would not be a good idea for him to be in his bedroll when Jim Langston arrives," said one of the men.

Bill stood and walked toward the camp and he greeted the two men.

“This is my camp, who are you, and who is Jim Langston?” asked Bill.

“We are scouts for the wagon train that is coming this way in the morning,” said one of the men.

“He is the wagon master for a convoy of wagons headed to California. There are about thirty wagons that will hold up here for a few days and you are camped right in the middle where those wagons stop.”

“Why do they have to stop at this point?” Bill would be happy to move his camp, he was curious as to why the wagon train stopped at this location. He could tell a lot of traffic had been through the area.

“The supply store is just on the other side of that hill, and Jim times his stops so he can get supplies here. The westbound wagons stop here, and the eastbound wagons stop over yonder a piece. The old wagon masters try to keep them separate. It is not a good thing for the eastbound people to be telling the westbound people all of their problems and why they are headed back home. So, there are two different spots. I have not heard of eastbound wagons on this trip, but it is not unusual.”

Bill began packing up his camp while the two scouts went after Grandy and Lou.

"Say you fellows have a pot we can boil water for coffee do you," Bill still looked forward to a cup of coffee.

"We sure do have a water pot. You kick up that fire a little, and I will get to the river and bring some water to put on to boil. We have some good Arbuckle coffee and I have been hankering for a cup all day," the scout mounted his horse and rode off in the direction of the river.

While the three men sat for a cup of coffee, Bill contemplated as to where to move his camp.

"You can set up over that little hill there. The outfitter store is a few hundred yards over there," said one of the scouts. "They have places all over where you can roll out your tarp. They are used to people setting up close to the store. The trappers have a Rendezvous every July over there. Last big shindig about three hundred showed up. That thing lasts as long as a week or two."

Bill thought to himself that here he was camped out with no coffee and he could have thrown a rock and hit the store where he could have bought a water pot. It was indeed strange how important some things became to a fellow living out by himself.

"Where are you two going to camp?" asked Bill.

"We are supposed to help get the wagons across the river so we will go back to find a spot on the bank. I may push this one into the river. He is getting a little ripe."

"You know better than that. I can't swim. I have told you that a hundred times, and you keep thinking about pushing me in the river. I do not stink near as much as you do, but I am going to find a shallow spot to throw some water on."

The two scouts mounted their horses and they were jawing with each other and laughing as they rode back in the direction of the river. Bill packed up and rode Grandy over the hill. Lazy Lou followed behind. He spotted the outfitter store. The large log cabin had been built up off the ground and it stood about fifty yards from the edge of a wooded area that led to the forest.

Bill found a spot behind the lodge where camps had been set a long time ago. He laid out his tarp and unrolled his blankets. He did not need a fire this late in the night, but he gathered some wood for the early morning fire.

The smell of coffee woke Bill and when he looked to see its source, he saw a very pretty young lady sitting on a log on the other side of a nice campfire. She had made a pot of coffee.

"Time to rise and shine, sleepyhead," the young woman said, grinning at Bill.

"Where did you come from, and where did you get the pot for coffee? Mine had holes all shot in it," said Bill.

"Nice to meet you too, mister," said the young woman. "My name is Julie and your best to remember I am the one that fixed your coffee. It is poured now and will likely be cold before you get your rear end out from under those blankets. And for where I come from, I live in this lodge with my mother and Trapper Kelly. So don't get any sideways ideas with me. I can probably shoot better than you anyway. Are you just going to sit there with your flycatcher wide open? I can come over there and pour that coffee in your mouth for you."

Julie rose from her seat with a cup in her hand, and Bill put his hand up to stop her.

"I am coming out of my blankets so you can stay right where you are," remarked Bill. He managed to throw off the blankets, knock his boots against each other to make sure no critters had crawled in during the night, and he sat with crossed legs to start sipping his coffee.

"This is really good coffee, Julie."

"Before you start getting all fresh and everything calling me by my name, you probably should tell me your name, and tell me what you are doing camped out here at our place," said Julie.

"My name is Bill Taylor. I am of a mind to make my home up in these mountains."

"What are you some kind of great trapper or something. Trappers are about all we see around here."

"No, I do not want to trap beaver. I just want to find a place so I can live in peace and I like the woods and the forest."

"My brother lives up in that mountain. He has a wife and two kids. My mother has it in her head that he will be coming down here soon. We have some supplies set aside for him," said Julie.

"That is what I am here for. I need to get some provisions before I head up in the mountain. This is a nice place. How long has it been here?"

"It has been here long enough for the wagon trains going both directions to know to stop here and we have a big to-do at the end of the trapping season every year. We stay busy. Where is your stuff and I will whip you up some breakfast?"

Bill finished his coffee and stood and brushed the dirt from his pants. His appearance had suddenly become important to him. He quickly put on his hat to cover his unruly hair. He had not shaved in months and he thought he probably looked like one of those rough old outlaws.

“Well, Miss Julie, I don’t have any stuff as you call it for breakfast. That is another thing on my list to get while I am here.”

“Come with me then, Mr. Bill, and we can go inside to meet my mother and Trapper Kelly, and we can share breakfast with you.”

The top of the sun had just begun to creep up and the rays announced a new day beginning. Bill followed Julie to the front of the building where they managed to get up some steps to a big porch. Julie swung open the front door.

“Mother, Trapper, we have company and I promised him some breakfast,” yelled Julie.

Bill stopped just inside the door. He did not see anyone inside until a woman came from a back room and walked with a quick step to where he stood.

“Welcome to Trapper Kelly’s Outfitter Lodge. I am Mary McCray. I see you have met my daughter Julie. Come in to our table. We have breakfast ready.”

“Thank you M’am. My name is Bill Taylor and I need to get some supplies before I move on.”

The three walked to the back of the store where a grizzled man sat at a long table. The man stood and held out his hand.

"I am Trapper Kelly. Friends just call me Trapper. I heard your name, and I think you said it was Bill Taylor, is that right?"

"Yes, it is my name. I am from Kentucky and I plan to head to the mountains," replied Bill.

"Do you happen to know a fellow from Kentucky that has that same last name as you? His name is Charlie Taylor. He is a good friend of mine."

"Charlie Taylor is my brother. I left home and he decided he wanted to farm. I understand that he now lives in Texas on a ranch there. My uncle is Frank Taylor and he has the bank in the little town of Live Oak Springs."

Trapper slapped Bill on the back and started he hawing like a donkey.

"You are like family here Bill. I declare the world gets just a little smaller every day. Sit down and plow in. I think we need to have some long talks."

Julie slid a plate in front of Bill. His breakfast consisted of two eggs, a large piece of ham. On another plate in front of him sat freshly bake biscuits and a slab of butter. Julie brought out a large bowl of cream gravy. Everyone buttered their biscuits and covered them with the cream gravy.

"I am going to have to take this in kind of slow. I have not eaten like this in a very long time," said Bill.

"Well, I for one think we need to fatten you up just a little. You are kind of skinny if you ask me," said Julie. Mary shushed Julie.

"You be polite, young lady. This just may be the way the man wants to look."

"Mother, I just don't think so. His buckskins are barely hanging on to those boney old hips. His clothes are too big. By the way, I know how to clean buckskin. If you will shed those clothes, I will get them looking brand new for you," Julie seemed to be a bit taken by this stranger named Bill.

He took his time getting around the breakfast fare and afterward, Trapper and Bill had a long talk about mountain life. Trapper told Bill that he needed someone to stay around for a while because he had grown old enough to rest in a rocking chair. Because of that, there were a lot of things that needed doing around the lodge that Mary and Julie could not take care of. The larder needed to be readied for the winter months, and that meant spending time in the forest hunting. While Trapper loved to hunt, he seemed to have lost the ability to stay out for long periods. He told Bill that he would take care of all his supplies if he could see his way clear to help around the lodge for a few weeks.

Bill thought Grandy and Lazy Lucy would benefit from an extended rest, and he could use the help with the supply bill.

10.

After thinking about Trapper's offer for a couple of days, Bill finally agreed to stay around the lodge for a while. He would see if he could hunt up enough meat for the stores in the smokehouse, and if there were some odds and ends to be taken care of, Bill thought he could handle everything. He had come to realize there were no deadlines for him to compete against. He could move anywhere he wanted and he could move at his own pace.

Julie had taken to hanging around Bill's campsite. She fixed meals for him over the campfire. She did take his buckskin pants and shirts to be cleaned, and that meant Bill had to stick around a while to get his clothes back. While he did not consider the possibility when he gave Julie the rolled-up dirty buckskins, Julie seemed to be purposely taking a slow time to get the clothes back to Bill.

"Miss Julie, I have to leave soon to go hunting to try to fill up your smokehouse. I will need my buckskins to go with me when I hunt. Do you know when you will be finished?" Bill asked.

Julie never answered, she would say something like, all in good time, and she encouraged patience.

Bill enjoyed the young woman's company and they conducted long conversations in the evenings.

"I would have thought a pretty young lady such as yourself would have found a man to marry by now. I do not mean you are getting long in the tooth or anything, but it surprises me that some fellow has not come in here and pulled on your heartstrings," observed Bill.

"I am a widow. A young man did earn my heart and we were married. He was killed by a gambler who came through here. My husband was not a card player and the gambler took advantage. A big fight happened and the gambler shot my husband and killed him. Another man involved killed the gambler, so there is that. I have had plenty of time to move through all that and I came back here to live with my mother in hopes of putting all that behind me."

"I am sorry, I should not have tried to look into your affairs," Bill's face reddened as he spoke quietly.

"It is alright, Bill. I have moved on and I look forward not backward. So, tomorrow, we are going to have to try out your shooting. If you are hunting for us, your eye needs to be clear, and your aim needs to be good. We have a place to shoot," Julie seemed to express confidence when she talked about the shooting.

"I am out of 52 caliber shells for my rifle. I hope the store carries those because that is why I came here in the first place. I will enjoy some shooting practice. Do you shoot?" asked Bill.

"I guess you will find out tomorrow. I think Trapper keeps a good stock of bullets that will work in that rifle of yours."

Early the next morning, Bill, Julie, and Trapper set out on foot to a nearby canyon. Bill wanted to check the sites on the long gun, Trapper had not been shooting in some time and Julie had hoped to get in some practice. Julie wore britches cinched up with a belt from one of her dresses. She had a cartridge belt with a holster strapped to her waist, and the holster fell low on her leg. Bill could see the handle of a gun at her fingertips. He had seen gunslingers with guns position just so.

Trapper carried a saddlebag loaded with ammunition. He had assured Bill there would be plenty of bullets for the Sharps rifle and for that pistol he wore.

Trapper had a 30 caliber lever-action Winchester rifle. He told Bill the Indian agents like to give the rifles to the Indians to make their hunting easier. Bill related to Trapper those Indians were using those rifles to try to kill soldiers, and while their skills were lacking, they made a day of it with the guns.

"Do you come down here a lot to get practice with a gun?" Bill asked Julie who walked beside him.

"I am here as often as I can be. I like shooting guns. I know that is not a female thing to do, but maybe that is why I like it. I like to ride horses, and I bet I can outride you, too."

While the canyon was small, it was deep enough so that there would be no fear of being hit with a ricochet. Several rock formations made perfect targets as they varied in round size from the smallest of about a foot diameter to some that were three feet across.

Trapper decided he would go first because all he wanted to do is make sure the Winchester shot true. He started on the biggest target and worked his way to the smallest. It appeared as though the gun sites were fine.

He turned to Bill and offered Bill an opportunity to step to a rock line on the ground. Bill, however, turned to Julie and told her to take her turn.

She stepped up to the rock line, drew her gun from her holster in a blur, and holding the gun in her right hand, she fanned the hammer until the gun cylinder was empty. She had shot at the smallest target and all six shots fell in a six-inch diameter circle in the middle of the target.

She turned to give Bill his turn and she saw the amazement on his face.

“What? Are you surprised or something? Better close your flycatcher mouth, Mr. Bill. I told you that I like to come here to do some shooting. Now it is your turn,” smiled Julie. Trapper stood behind Bill with a grin on his face.

“I have never, I mean, I did not know a gun would shoot like that,” said Bill.

“No, what you mean is you never saw a female shoot a gun like that. Now you have, so you better get over yourself. Wait, just step back a little bit. I do not think I am through just yet.” Julie had reloaded her gun, stepped back up to the firing line, and proceeded to calmly shoot all six shots again. This time she held the gun out straight with her right hand and she placed her left hand under the butt of the pistol for support. Of course, she shot the same target until it started to crumble.

“I guess you probably thought that is how a female should be able to shoot,” said Julie.

"Honestly, I have never seen a female shoot a gun, much less pull a fast draw and fan that pistol the way you did, and you hit the target to boot. That is the best shooting I have ever seen, man or woman," said Bill shaking his head. He turned on his heel and took a few steps heading back out of the canyon.

"Wait up, Bill. You have not had a chance to practice your shooting, yet," called Trapper.

Bill realized he had been stunned by Julie's shooting exhibition. When he returned and stepped to the firing line, he methodically shot at the big target with his rifle and worked his way down to the smallest. He could see a small piece of the smallest rock target still standing. He took a shot and the target disappeared.

"You can shoot good enough to go hunting for us, I think. What about you Trapper? You think he can bring home enough to fill our smokehouse?" asked Julie. "If you do not think he can do it, I will go out again this year. I filled it up last year and the year before, and I know I can do it again."

"Let us give Bill the go-ahead, and you can go out if he comes in short. How is that, Julie?" Trapper knew he did not have to ask because Julie had told him she was disappointed to not go hunting this year.

"I tell you what, Bill. If it is fine with my mother, I will go out with you. That way we will pack up enough food to last us the winter for sure," Julie smiled at the idea and hurried back to the lodge to clear the hunting trip with her mother.

Bill and Trapper picked up all of the empty shells on the ground and found a small round rock to replace the one that got shattered during the target practice.

"I have never had anyone go with me on a hunting trip, Trapper," Bill had a concerned look on his face.

"Oh, I think it is a good idea for Julie to go along. She knows the land and it will save a bunch of time because she has a good idea of where the deer and the elk lay up. I have no doubt the two of you can get us through the winter. It would be nice to get some fat turkey also. I have an old shotgun I will send along so you will have it in case you come across some."

By the time the two men reached the outfitter lodge, Julie had cleared the hunting trip with her mother, and she started packing the gear she would need for the trip.

Two big bags were resting on the front porch when Bill and Trapper came up the steps.

"I see Julie got the go-ahead from Mary to go hunting. She keeps these bags ready all the time just in case we need her to go out."

"I am still not sure about all this, Trapper. Maybe she could go in one direction and I could go to the other. That way we will have twice as good a chance of finding game," said Bill.

"You could do that, I guess," replied Trapper. "But one of you could get shot by the other one. And the quicker you get to where the game is located, the quicker you can return. I see you out for about a week is all."

"Well, if you think it would go that quick, I will be willing to give it a try," Bill said. "I have never had a partner hunting before."

"Yeah, you said that already, Bill," grinned Trapper.

11.

Bill had Grandy saddled when Julie came around the building with her mustang. Lazy Lou followed closely behind.

"What is it with this mule of yours? When I got my horse saddled, your mule stood so close to me I had a hard time moving around," Julie had an exasperated look on her face.

"I do not know what is going on with Lazy Lou. I guess he likes you or something," Bill replied. When he started walking toward the mule with the packs, Lazy Lou started backing up. "That is a first. This mule has never shied from a pack before."

"Let me have it and we will just see what this mule is up to," said Julie.

She picked up the packs and Lazy Lou walked up beside her. She managed to throw the packs over the back of the mule.

"Now I have seen everything. Lazy Lou has been with me since we left Kentucky and he has never acted that way," said a surprised Bill.

"Who names a mule Lazy Lou anyway?" asked Julie. "You need to come up with a better name. Maybe that is the problem. Your horse and this mule are going to have a hard time in the forest. My little mustang will be able to scat around real good."

"We have spent plenty of time in the forest. Grandy is good at picking out trails, and Lazy Lou just follows along. I do not even put a lead rope on him."

"Since I know where we are going, I will take the lead. It will take us a day to get close to a park and we will need to camp there," Julie gave her mustang a nudge and she started him up the mountainside. Bill was surprised at the wide trail.

"This trail will go a long way up the mountain. We have worked on it for several years to make it easy to travel. We will be turning off west after about half the day is gone. That trail will be a hard one. We have some narrow pathways on the side of a cliff to get by. I like to walk that one just in case," Julie continued in the lead.

Bill marveled at how much Julie had explored the mountain. She had become familiar enough to hunt and bag enough game to last the family during the cold winter months.

Around midday, Julie pulled up and motioned for Bill to come up beside her. She reached in a saddlebag that she had tied on behind her saddle and she brought out several pieces of jerky.

"Here is lunch. Eat a few of these and they should last you until we get settled in camp," Julie handed Bill some of the jerky and she nudged her mustang forward.

Julie presented a different attitude when she went on the hunt. Bill noticed she took charge of everything, and she had a particular way of getting things done. When they reached the cutoff that would lead them to the park, Julie stopped and explained the track to Bill.

"I want you to know about this place because we might get separated and you may need to find your way out of here. It can get a little dark in here even though it is daytime. The trees grow so close together, they let in very little light. You have to watch for deadfall. My mustang knows this track pretty well, but you may be a little blind in here. If you start feeling like you are falling behind, send up a shout and I will come back for you.

Lazy Lou has been following me up till now, but I think he needs to be behind you. Keep him close, we do not want to lose our supplies."

While Bill was not accustomed to taking direction from a female, he felt very comfortable with the instructions Julie handed out. She knew the place, and she knew how to get where they needed to go to find game.

After making the turn into the narrow track, Bill got an idea of why Julie gave such a forceful description. Darkness set in about fifty yards in on the trail. He could barely make out Julie's back and the mustang's rear end. They were only twenty yards ahead of him. Lazy Lou trailed close behind Grandy. It did not take long for Bill to lose sight of Julie. He did not panic because he felt they were on the same trail and he felt he would eventually be able to see her. That worked out nice until he came to a fork in the trail and he did not have any idea which way Julie had gone. It came time for him to let out a yell. Julie answered for him to stay where he was and she would come to get him.

After a few anxious minutes, Bill saw Julie appear out of the darkness. She walked toward him and put her hand on Grandy's shoulder.

"How is everything back here, Bill? I forgot to tell you to take the left fork. My mustang is up there a way, I did not want to take the trouble to try to turn him around on this narrow trail. I will walk with you until we catch up with him. He probably just kept walking on," said Julie.

She kept her hand on Grandy's shoulder as they walked to the left fork on the trail and continued in the darkness.

"How did you ever find this place where we are going?" asked Bill.

"I love the forest and I love exploring. I found this and I brought Trapper up here with me a few times. He thinks it is too dangerous to go to all this trouble, but when we get to the park, you will see why I like this way. Just stay with me and we will be just fine," Julie kept walking.

Bill did not have any fear about where they were or where they were going, he liked to have a plan, and he knew Julie had a plan, but he had no idea what that plan might be.

They passed the place where she had left her horse. Bill asked her if she wanted to ride and he could walk for a bit.

"I have walked this whole trip before. The first few times I came up here, a horse could not get through here, so I can walk it," said Julie.

"How did you ever get your game out of here?" asked Bill.

"Well, that was a chore, I will tell you. I brought one of the sleds the trappers use to haul pelts, but I had several loads. I would have to drag that thing so far, unload it, and go back for the rest. It took me nearly a week to get out of here. I had left my horse back at the wide track and I sure was happy when I got there."

Bill continued to be amazed at what Julie had accomplished. She had already done more with her life in the mountains than he could in several years. He had respect and admiration for her.

"There is a little spot up here where the sun finally breaks through. I am pretty sure that is where we will find my horse because the grass grows there. It will be a good spot to stop for a little rest for Grandy and Lazy Lou."

When they reached the spot where the sun shined, Bill had to blink to adjust his eyes to the brightness. He dismounted and turned Grandy and Lazy Lou to graze awhile.

He sat next to Julie who had found a big fallen tree that made a perfect seat.

"The next part of our trip gets a little scary. We are going to skirt a bluff where the drop off is about thirty feet down into a heavily wooded canyon. There is a stream in there that carries the snowmelt from the higher elevations. That stream can get very noisy at spots where it travels over big boulders. I have been down there and looked at it, but it is not a place where we want to go right now. There is a rock outcrop on the edge of that bluff that we have to walk on to get around to the other side. It is wide enough for us and the horses, but if you look down, it kind of messes with your head. I keep my eyes looking straight ahead because I need to watch my step. The horses can get a little nervous on that narrow edge, but we should be able to make it fine. Coming back will be a cinch since they have already seen it. Just know there will be no turning around because once we are on that ledge, there is only one way to go. The ledge is only about a hundred yards long, but there is a turn in the middle and we may lose sight for a short time."

"Maybe we should have taken that fork to the right and got passed all this stuff," said Bill.

"Nope, that would have led us around until we wound up smack in the middle of an Indian village. And that is a place you do not want to be. I would rather be at the bottom of that canyon." Julie stood up signaling the brief rest had ended.

"I want to put your mule behind my mustang. I don't think he will get as nervous as he would walking behind Grandy. My mustang is used to this ledge and he will be fine. That should give Lazy Lou a bit of security."

Julie led her mustang to the ledge with Lazy Lou trailing behind. She looked back over her shoulder to make sure Bill and Grandy were ready and she took off.

Everyone made the trip on the ledge just fine. Bill did hear rushing water about midway through, but he heeded Julie's advice and kept his eyes forward.

When they stepped off the ledge onto firm ground, Bill let out a big breath.

"I did not know I was holding my breath all that way," Bill said. "I think I might have lost a year or two back there."

"I know I did the first time I went around there. A bobcat had perched himself just around the turn. I made enough noise that he took off. I never figured where he went," said Julie. "We are close to the park and we want to set camp up to make sure we are downwind. It will not be long before we get to see all the game we can handle."

Julie unrolled a big tarp from her heavy bag. She tied four corners to the trees and let the big leftover flap fold down to the ground. Enough tarp stretched out on the ground so she would have enough room to put her bedroll down. It became clear to Bill that Julie had a lot of experience making a hunting camp.

Julie stretched rope about head high from one tree to another so they would have a place to hang the game they harvested. Another rope went from one tree to another in front of her lean-to. She put up another small tarp which gave her privacy in her makeshift room.

Bill put a circle of rocks down for a fire pit and he had a small fire blazing in short order. He asked Julie if there happened to be a stream nearby where they could get water. Julie took Bill's hand and walked him over to a small brook where the water ran swift and clear. He managed to get enough water to set to boil so they could make coffee. When they returned to the camp, Julie ran a small grass rope around several trees making a small corral for the horses and mule.

"If they want out of there, they can get out. But, it is easy to keep them nearby while we hunt. There is a good spot for them to graze out in the park, but we can put them out there during the day so they will not scare off our game. After we have some coffee, I think we should sneak out to the edge of the woods and watch what happens out there when the sun starts going down," Julie poured coffee into two tin cups and handed one to Bill.

"You do enjoy being out here, don't you?" Bill asked.

"I do enjoy being here. I love the forest, the animals, and just being here. Usually, I am here by myself, but I kind of like having a little company along," replied Julie.

Bill had become used to wearing his moccasins and when they walked to the edge of the forest, he did so quietly. Julie had worn moccasins also. Their walk did not alarm anything.

They found another log that had fallen in a perfect place for them to sit and look out upon a vast park. A stream ran down from the higher elevations and disappeared into the forest. As the sun began to set, Bill saw a huge herd of deer enter the park from the northwest side of the river. He guessed there were about fifty deer lazily grazing and working their way to the water. All of the deer managed to get a drink from the stream when something alerted them. Heads turned in the same direction as the deer sniffed the air to get a scent of something that seemed to be coming their way. A nervous buck in the back of the herd flipped his tail up and the herd ran to the woods where they had come out. There were so many deer, Bill could hear their hooves striking the ground. He looked to see what might have frightened them, but he could not make anything out. Julie nudged him with her elbow and pointed to a place that was on the northeast side of the river. A big elk ambled out into the park. He stomped around, turning in a circle and he ran back into the woods.

"There is something on our side that is scaring them. It could be a bear or a mountain lion or something, but I do not see it. If it pokes its head out to where we can see it, I think we should take it," said Julie.

After a little time had passed, a cat about the size of a bobcat stealthily made its way to the stream.

“That looks like a bobcat. I am surprised he scared the elk and deer away, “said Bill.

“That is a Lynx,” said Julie. “They are a little larger than a bobcat because their legs are longer and they are really fast. If we get one, take a look at its feet, they are very big. I think we let that fellow drink. There will be more game out here in a bit.”

Bill and Julie sat on the log until darkness overcame. They witnessed more deer, elk, and even moose coming to water. They enjoyed the show when a bear tried his hand at fishing in the stream. The bear would pounce on a fish and try to hold it while it flopped enough to get free. After a couple of failed attempts, the bear appeared to give up. As he walked along on the bank of the stream, he gave a fish one last try. This time the bear threw the fish on the ground and pounced on it with both paws. He had finally managed to get something to eat.

“Those bear are going to be really active now because it will not be long before hibernation time for them. They have to put on a lot of fat to get them through the winter months. It is kind of like we are going to have to fatten you up so you can make it through the winter. The weather up here can be mean, and it takes a lot to prepare for the cold weather.

After their meal at camp, Julie hung a spare blanket on the rope she had stretched across the front of the lean-to.

"I am staying in here, and I expect you to stay out there," said Julie.

"I had no other thought," replied Bill.

Bill made his bed on pine boughs and he used his saddle blanket for a pillow. He sat by the fire for a time, thinking about the day's events. He heard a little snore coming from the area where Julie had put her bed.

"I think this is just about as good as I have ever had it," Bill thought to himself. He looked over to the corral and saw the horses were calm, and he felt it time for him to get some sleep.

12.

"If they show up, I think we should take as many deer as we can this morning. All the shooting will scare the rest of the game away, but we will have plenty of work for us until the evening. Most of them will forget about the morning shooting, and come right back to water in the evening. I have Trapper's rifle and you have yours. I figure we should be able to take two each before they all disappear. If we can get more, then that is even better," Julie laid out the plan for the day over a breakfast of eggs and bacon. Bill thought if he kept eating the way he had been eating since he came to the lodge that he would be laying on the fat like one of those hibernating bears.

Julie took a spot about fifty yards north of where Bill set up. They waited for the deer to come in to graze and get a drink of water. At the first shot, they all took off on a run to the woods for shelter. Bill managed to get two, and Julie fired three shots and took three deer. They returned to camp to get the mustang and Lazy Lou to haul the carcasses to the camp for processing. Bill hobbled the horses and mule so they could graze out in the park while he and Julie processed the deer. By the time he returned to camp, Julie had finished with the second deer and started on number three. Bill stood and watched her make quick work of processing the deer.

After cutting some backstrap for their meal, she salted them and wrapped all three in burlap. Bill took the hides and put them on a makeshift stretcher for them to dry.

They had stopped for a brief lunch and went back to work. They had finished with the morning take by dusk.

"We best move a little south of where we were this morning if we plan to get any elk," said Julie. "They will come into water, but they will not be as comfortable as the deer were this morning. I would like to see us get one each, and then we can take care of that tonight.

By the end of the week, Bill and Julie had more than enough meat to fill up the smokehouse at the lodge. They packed up and while they had used a lot of the supplies they packed in, they replaced the weight and added more for Lazy Lou to carry. The mule had taken to shying away from Bill, so Julie had to strap down the packs. Lazy Lou seemed content to have Julie put as much weight on as she could lift. If Bill came over to help, the mule would sidestep into a complete circle to stay away from him.

"I don't know where you found that cantankerous old mule, but I think I may have found me a new best friend," grinned Julie.

"You can sure have him. I am about done with the thing. That mule acted just fine when I got him. He has done well all through that scouting job with the military until we got to the outfitter lodge. That is when he started throwing these little fits and not letting me put packs on him. When we get back down to the lodge, I am going to see if I can still ride him. Lazy Lou has a real easy gate, and he can go for days without stopping."

They navigated the treacherous ledge with very little problem. Julie had put Lazy Lou behind the maverick again and Bill watched the mule match every move the mustang made. They stopped for a rest at the little sunshine area before entering the dark forest.

Even that section of the trail seemed to be much easier to get through and when they broke out of the darkness into the wide track that would lead them down the mountain to the outfitter lodge, Bill began to relax and he enjoyed the ride.

When they arrived at the lodge, they filled the smokehouse larder and planned to turn the riding stock loose in the corral. Bill and Julie were brushing the horses when a young man made his way into the barn.

"August," Julie shouted. "Oh, it is so good to see you. My goodness, you have really grown up. Meet Bill Taylor. He and I just got back from a hunt and he can really shoot."

The young man looked a Bill and extended his hand to shake Bill's hand. "Good to meet you, sir. My name is August and I am Julie's brother. She sometimes gets excited about stuff and forgets who I am."

"Where is Boots? How long have you been here? Did Migisi and Little Boots come along too?" Julie asked rapid-fire questions.

"Boots is in the lodge. We have been here two days, and no, Migisi stayed with her mother and she kept Little Boots and Ayashe with her," August answered. He looked over at Bill with an apologetic look on his face. "Those are people we will have to tell you about. Boots is my big brother. His real name is July, but our mother named him Boots. He was born in July and his father named him. I have a sister named June who is older than Julie, and you can guess when she was born. Then there is Julie.

I would think you could figure out her birthday month. Now, with my name being August, if you have not figured all this out by now, I think you might be a little short in the head," August smiled at Bill.

"Give me those brushes and you two can go to the house to see Boots. I will finish up with these two. That is a nice horse you have there," said August as he admired Grandy.

"His name is Grandy because he is a grand horse," replied Bill as he handed the brush to the young man.

Bill and Julie climbed the steps to get to the porch of the lodge. Julie opened the door and burst into the room to embrace her brother.

Boots reached around Julie to shake Bill's hand.

"I am Boots McCray, it is good to meet you. My mother and Trapper have been telling me about you. I am glad you found this place. They will need you here for as long as you want to stay.

Boots had on clothes that fitted a mountain man. He wore a head covering made from beaver pelt. His buckskin shirt showed intricate beadwork. There were pockets sewed to the front of his buckskin pants and those pockets contained intricate beadwork. Mary noticed Bill taking in the clothes that Boots wore.

My daughter in law Migisi is a Cheyenne. She is responsible for the garments that Boots has on. She does some good work don't you think?" Mary asked.

"Yes, it makes my clothes look rather plain. They are nice," remarked Bill. "I want to sit and talk with Boots about his time in the mountains. I came to this country to head up in the mountains and I want to know firsthand what I should expect.

"Have a seat, Bill, and I will try to answer every question you can think of. Julie, could you get us some coffee and, I think mother is bringing out some food for us. So, we have all the time in the world to talk about the mountains."

Bill was enthused to be able to talk with Boots. He had an idea about mountain life, but he wanted to know the straight of it from someone who lives it. His first question to Boots was about where he lived.

Their discussion went well into the night. Trapper and Mary retired for the evening. Julie and August were at the table listening to the two men talk. Boots started a yawn and Bill realized the late hour and he had not set up his camp. He told Boots that he hoped they could continue to talk in the morning.

When Bill left the lodge building, he walked around to where his first camp had been set. He had dropped his camp packs there and he did not look forward to unpacking everything and setting up camp so late at night. When he rounded the corner of the building, he first saw a campfire that had been lit some time ago because the coals were showing red and small flames were caught on branch pieces. When he got closer, he saw August and Julie unloading packs and setting up his camp.

"You two do not have to do that. I know you are both tired. I can take care of things from here, so you can go find your blankets," said Bill.

"We have our blankets already," said August. "We are staying out here with you. Julie has your bedroll laid out and we were just waiting for you so we could get to sleep." Bill thanked August and Julie for setting up camp. He went to bed thinking he had found some nice people.

13.

Bill woke to the slamming of the door to the smokehouse. Trapper had been inside inspecting the haul that Bill and Julie brought in the evening before. When he kicked back his blankets, he noticed Julie and August were already up and gone.

Trapper sat on a stump near the burned down campfire.

"I think Boots is going to see if you want to go up to his place with him," said Trapper. "I would like for you to think hard on that before you decide to go. There is a young lady in that lodge that has her cap set for you. What I want you to think about is, what would your going up in the mountain do to her. I know you had no idea about Julie's feelings. That is why I am here this morning telling you about them."

"I had no idea, Trapper," replied Bill. "I do not have any experience with females, and I did not read that in her. We sure enjoyed each other's company on that hunting trip and we made a very good team. I guess I would have to say I am very fond of Julie. That may not even be a strong enough word."

"It sounds to me like there is something to make of the two of you may be being together. I know if you take off with Boots, Julie is likely to want to go along with you two. I know her mother wants her here. She knows Julie can take care of herself, but she is Julie's mother and it may not make a lot of sense to us, but Mary wants her daughter close to home."

"I can guess I can understand that," replied Bill. "That sure puts a different light on my thinking. What would you do if you were me?"

"I had already opened this store up before Boots brought his family up here. I could have left this store for them to take care of, but I chose to stay here. When we have business in that store, those people come to see Mary and Julie. They don't come to see me. Since they have come here, we have made money enough so that we could close up that store and live nicely in some town somewhere. But we are staying here because we want to."

Bill's attitude turned a little quiet during the day, while he thought about the conversation he had with Trapper. He stayed mostly by himself, avoiding Boots and Julie completely. He and August fed the livestock and cleaned out the stalls in the barn, but that was about it. Bill wandered on foot up into the forest. He found a rock bench where he could sit and look over the land where the outfitter lodge building sat. He began to realize that he had come to like it at the lodge. Bill asked himself the question if he liked the lodge because Julie lived there. He admitted that played a big part in why he considered staying.

Bill heard rustling in the woods behind him and when he turned to look, he saw Boots making his way to the rock bench.

"I see you found the thinking bench. Trapper told me about his conversation with you this morning, and I have been thinking about it ever since. I would be happy to take you up the mountain to my home. Winter will be setting in within a few weeks and it snows a lot up there. The weather is just about as edgy as it can get. When it snows, we are snowed in. There is the possibility that we could get snowed in while we are up there and you could not make it back down here until the thaw in the spring. That is something to think about.

Julie has had a rough go of it for most of her life. She married a fellow and they were happy for a short time until the fellow got himself killed. It has taken her a long time to work through all of that stuff, and your coming along when you did has sure gotten her eyes sparkling again. I know she feels strongly for you. I hope you have strong feelings for her because she sure does not need to be hurt right now. You know that if we took off up that mountain that she would be right alongside us. She has been to our home before. So she knows the tough parts of it. I am telling you this because I think you are an upright fellow and we don't get to see too many upright fellows out here. Most of them are running from the law or they are working for the fur buying company. It is your decision about what you want to do, and if you take off tomorrow, we will be sad about it, but we would not hold it against you."

Boots stood up and put his hand on Bill's shoulder and squeezed. He turned and left Bill with his thoughts. He stayed on the rock bench for most of the day.

As the sun started to sink, Bill heard some more noise behind him. He turned to see Julie making her way to the rock bench.

"I was just thinking we could probably have a parade up here," Bill grinned at Julie.

"I came to let you know that we will have supper soon and I want to know if I can help you. It seems as though you have been troubled all day, and I am pretty good at sorting things out. I would like to be able to help you with your thoughts, if you let me that is," Julie looked into Bill's eyes. He continued to look at her.

"That is going to be a pretty tall order because you a mixed up in a bunch of this mess and I am not sure you will be able to get clear of it enough to be able to help a fellow through his thoughts. I do not have troubles, let me say. I probably have the best situation a man could have. I am just trying to think my way through how I should handle myself," said Bill.

"There you have it. You see I am somewhat smart about things like that. I can tell you how to handle yourself in just about any situation. Now you have to tell me the situation so I can set you straight."

"Julie the situation is exactly this. I came out here to live in the mountains away from everything and everybody. I wanted the peace and quiet of the forest and the mountains. Now here I find myself having some strong feelings for a pretty young lady. I am thinking over maybe I will not go up in the mountains to find peace and quiet, because I just may find something better if I stay right where I am now. How would a fellow comport himself in that situation, I ask." Bill turned and saw a tear rolling down Julie's cheek. He used his thumb to wipe it away. "Now see what I have done. I have started that pretty young lady tearing up and bawling. I did not want that to happen. You better come across quick like with how I am supposed to handle myself."

"Right now, Bill Taylor, you are handling yourself just about perfect. Not quite perfect yet, but pretty close. I am no bawling. That was a tear of happiness. I enjoyed what you said to me because I pretty well have some strong feelings for you as well. If I hear you right, you are thinking about giving up your life ambition to live in the mountains so that you could stay here with me. Do I have that pretty close to right?

"I believe you are closer to being on the money than when you were shooting targets. Now how do we manage to get through all this?" asked Bill.

"I know that Boots thought you might want to go up to his home at the cave. If you go, I will go with you. If you want a home in the mountains, I will go with you. I can hunt and shoot. I can live in the mountains and be happy. If that is what you want, we can pack and be gone in the morning."

"Well, see here now, there are some other matters to consider. Trapper wants me to stay around here and help with the lodge and such. And I know your mother wants you close at hand. I am pretty sure you would like to stay close to your mother as well. So, how do we handle all that?"

Julie became quiet as she thought about what Bill had just said. She did want to stay close to her mother, and she knew her mother wanted her close at hand. She told her as much when Julie returned home after the death of her husband.

"We can get this figured out. I like the sound of that we thing. We are a good team and together, we can get just about anything figured. It has been just one day. We can think about it some more and we can come up with some ideas. Now, you are going to have to hold my hand when we walk back down to the lodge for supper. That is a requirement, Bill Taylor, so get up from there and take my hand."

The evening meal was quiet. Very little conversation took place and most of that centered on chores that needed to be cleared up the next day. Boots had taken August into a nearby town to get him outfitted with a new set of clothes and they planned to spend the night at the local hotel. Julie had decided to stay in her room inside the lodge. Bill had moved his blankets to the storage room where a makeshift bunkhouse had been set up. It would mark the first night in several years that Bill slept inside and not under the stars. He had a restless night and he finally decided to get up early.

He stoked the campfire and put water on for coffee. He thought he heard a tinkling sound like glass breaking. He did not hear anything else, so he thought maybe he imagined the noise.

A few minutes later, he heard a scream and he knew it was Julie who screamed. He quickly put on his boots and grabbed his gun belt. He stepped up onto the front porch of the lodge and he saw one of the windows in the door broken. It confirmed that he did hear glass breaking. The door stood open a few inches so Bill pushed it open and stepped into the store. He could see some activity in the back of the building so he crouched down and duck walked down one of the aisles until he reached the disturbance.

A strange man had his arm around Julie's throat. She had both hands on that arm and she was scratching hard enough blood started seeping. Bill's anger started to overtake him. Nobody had a right to treat anybody the way that man was treating Julie. Especially Julie. Trapper stood in front of Mary, but he did not have a weapon. He tried to talk the man into letting Julie go. The man was having none of it.

Julie had been sound asleep in her bed when the man entered her room and grabbed her by the front of her nightclothes. He pulled her up out of bed and he tried to kiss her. Julie could smell whiskey on the man's breath and she slapped him across the face. The fellow did not expect a fight. He turned Julie around and held her with his arm around her throat.

"You can just calm down Missy. We can have us a little party. I am pretty sure you will have some fun too. Now we are going to back out of here and I am taking you to my camp. I have everything fixed just so for you there," the man whispered in her ear.

Julie stomped her foot on the top of the man's boot. She was not wearing shoes, but still, it had some effect. The man started hopping on one foot trying to back out of her room. Trapper had heard the commotion and he had just come out of his room when the man had Julie in the hallway. He continued to back out into the store. Trapper knew he could not let the man leave with Julie. He happened to see Bill come through the front door. Bill had managed to get behind the man without him knowing it. Bill put his arm around the man's throat.

"You will take your hands off this young woman right now," Bill said forcefully.

"I ain't gonna do that. This here hen is mine and I am taking her with me. You let go of me or she might get hurt."

Bill put the barrel of his gun against the man's head.

"I hope you get the idea of letting her go now," Bill said as he cocked the pistol the click sounded loud.

"There ain't no need for any shootin'. We all know what these women are good for and I am just takin' my turn. You can put that gun down and I will give you a turn with her when I am finished."

The man was telling Bill Taylor exactly the wrong thing. Bill squeezed his arm muscle so tight against the man's neck that the fellow started passing out.

Julie felt the man's grip on her neck loosen and she pulled away from him. When she was clear of the man, Bill brought the butt of his pistol down hard on the man's head knocking him out cold.

Bill grabbed Julie in an embrace.

"Are you alright? Are you hurt?" Bill stood back and held her at arm's length as he looked over her from head to toe. Julie had her hands on his arms. Tears flowed over her cheeks."

"I am fine now. I am not hurt, but I am angry," replied Julie. "How did that man get in here? Where did he come from?"

Trapper stood over the intruder as he tied his hands behind his back and his feet were tied together. Trapper ran the rope around the man's ankles to the rope binding his hands. He looped it over and pulled it tight, causing the man's knees to bend and his feet came almost up to his hands. The man was hogtied.

Bill walked over and looked in the man's face. He recognized the fellow as being one of the men that had shot holes in his water pot. Bill thought for a moment. The man's name was either Ray or Sam, he could not remember, but he could remember there were two of them. They were headed east and he came west. They must have changed direction. Bill could not remember much about them, other than they were hungry and he gave them food.

"As soon as this one wakes up, I am taking him to town to meet the Sheriff," said Trapper. He found some water left on the stove. It had cooled enough that Trapper threw the water in the man's face.

"Wake up you scoundrel," said Trapper as the man started trying to move. "I ought to take you out and shoot you for coming in here and doing what you did to Julie." Trapper brought his foot back to kick the man in the stomach.

"Don't do it, Trapper," said Julie. "Let him be. If anybody needs to do any kicking it is me, and I do not want to right now." Julie had pulled Bill into an embrace and her head rested on his chest.

The man on the floor began to regain his faculties and started moaning. Bill had Julie step back as he walked over to the man. He looked at the face of Julie's assailant. He glowered at the fellow.

"If you were standing upright about now, I would beat you until they buried you," Bill's anger continued to build. "You are the worst of the worst. I don't know where you came from, but you better tell me where your partner is right now."

"I am standing right here," Bill heard the voice coming from the front of the store. He looked up to see the partner pointing a pistol at him. "I think you best stand up and move over there with the rest of the folks so I can keep an eye on you." The man used his gun to motion Bill over to where Julie, Trapper, and Mary stood.

14.

"Sam, what have you gotten yourself into now?" the man named Ray asked.

"I just come in here asking for a bite to eat and that feller over there decided to pistol whip me. They tied me up while I was sleeping. They were gonna rob me, Ray. Thank goodness you came in when you did. I am in a bind here. Can't you figure how to untie me and let me loose?" Sam rolled around on the floor trying to loosen the knots on the rope.

Julie stepped forward with an angry look on her face.

"That man is lying through the few teeth he has. He came in here and pulled me out of my bed thinking he would take me to your camp. Bill put that knot on his head because he was trying to drag me out of here," Julie started shaking as she stood in her ripped nightclothes.

"That just don't sound like my buddy Sam. One of you people needs to get over here and cut him loose. We will be out of your hair pretty quick. There is no need for anybody to get hurt, but this gun can shoot," Ray stood in the doorway. He could see Sam on the floor, but while he was looking at him, Trapper went out the back door and around to the front of the lodge. "I think I am taking his story over yours. If you people took his money, you better give it back."

A loud click sounded in the store as Trapper cocked the shotgun he had pointed at Ray's back. "I hope you heard that," said Trapper. "That was just one barrel of this double-barrel shotgun I have pointed at your back." Another click sounded. "That is the other barrel of this loaded shotgun. I will blow you into yesterday unless you throw that gun down."

Ray let the gun fall to the floor and he put his hands up in the air.

"Now, kick that gun over to the side," instructed Trapper.

Ray did as he was told and Bill walked up to Ray.

"I guess I should have shot you two instead of giving you food. We would not be here right now if I had done what I should have done back in that park," Bill got to within inches of Ray's face. "You fools followed me here?"

"Naw, we have been lost for several weeks. We just camped over on the other side of the river. Sam likes the taste of liquor, and I think he had a few too many sips. I will just untie him and take him back to camp," said Ray.

"The only place you two are going is to town to meet the Sheriff. I know he will have a nice place for you to stay," said Trapper. He leaned the shotgun against the wall and tied Ray's hands behind his back.

"If I remember just right, Ray told me that the law is looking for him, so I am pretty sure the Sheriff will be more than glad to see him," Bill said.

Bill and Trapper found the camp where the two men were staying. It happened to be just over the little hill and in the area where the westward-bound wagon trains circled for their stay. They gathered the belongings, tied the men to their horses, and headed into the nearby town to turn them over to the law.

They passed Boots and August on the trail to town, and they related the incident to them. When Boots and August arrived at the lodge, they found Julie in her room in tears, and Mary shook from what had occurred just hours earlier.

The law had been hunting for Ray since he had been identified as having robbed a bank in California. A worker in the bank had been shot and killed during the robbery. A five hundred dollar reward had been offered for his capture.

Sam had been sought out on a vagrancy charge. It seems he liked to sleep on the streets of towns and he would either pick the pockets of people or just outright relieve them of their valuables. While the law wanted him arrested, there had been no reward money posted for Sam. He felt disappointed.

After getting back to the outfitter lodge and having their noon lunch, Boots and Bill walked about the grounds talking about what had happened.

"I came out here to try to deal with me getting mad at people. I thought if I just got away from people, I would not have any reason to get angry. I felt the mountains would be a good cure for that problem. But, I am finding that I can get angry with anything. I am mad at that mule over there," Bill looked at Lazy Lou. "I am not mad enough to do anything about it, I am just mad at Lazy Lou." Bill recounted the story about the mule acting just fine until the animal got around Julie.

"Bill, mules, horses, cows, and dogs can all see things in us that we cannot begin to understand. That old mule over there sees something in Julie that we cannot see and he wants to be around her and do her bidding. I know that seems a little strange, but that is the way things are. I can sure understand your anger over those two characters who messed with us here this morning, and I think you have handled yourself rather capital in that entire affair. You have probably already solved the matter and do not even know it yet. When a colt is born they are a little rowdy as they discover their legs, and the whole world is a fun place. Now look at Grandy and as you think back to Grandy as a newborn colt, think about the way Grandy handles himself today. Time has grown that horse into a smarter way of thinking. Reckon that might have happened to you?"

Bill thought a long time about what Boots said.

"I guess that living up there in the mountains gives you a little more clear-headed thinking about things," said Bill. "Down here there is so much going on things can get all jumbled up in your head and sometimes there is no one clear way to think about stuff."

"That is one way to look at it, and I think as we grow a little older every day, things become a little clearer."

Bill walked back to the lodge and when he entered through the front door he noticed the double-barrel shotgun leaning against the wall. He picked the gun up and broke open the barrel.

"No wonder those clicks sounded so loud. There are no shotgun shells in this gun. It was not even loaded. Did you know that Trapper?" asked Bill.

"Yes, I knew it was not loaded, but that idiot standing in front of it did not know there weren't any shells in that gun. It worked is all I can say. I am glad he did not know guns very well, or he would have noticed the gun was empty with those loud clicks when I pulled the triggers back." Trapper grinned at Bill.

Later in the day, a band of Cheyenne braves came to the lodge. A young woman and two children were riding horses in the back of the group.

Boots walked out on the porch and smiled when he saw Migisi, Little Books, and Ayashe. They had been escorted to the lodge by ten young braves and an older man.

"I have brought my daughter and grandchildren to you. We are going back to our village now," the older Indian turned his horse and rode to where Migisi stayed mounted on her horse. They had a conversation in the Cheyenne language and the escorts rode away in a gallop.

Migisi helped her daughter from her horse as Little Boots slid off his mustang and ran to his father. August appeared and he took the ropes of the three horses to lead them to the barn and corral. He noted there were no saddles, just a blanket on the back of the horses.

Bill stood quietly as he was introduced to Boots' family. He admired Boots for accomplishing a dream of living in the mountains and raising a fine family.

The End

Made in United States
Orlando, FL
26 April 2023